E
E
Cla.
Eaglesi
Giffnock.

Hollie Hughes & Leigh Hodgkinson

The FAMISHING vanishing mAHOOSIVE mammoth

BLOOMSBURY
LONDON OXFORD NEW YORK NEW DELHI SYDNEY

A maHOOSIVE
mammoth
one morning awoke
    and groaned to his friend,
"My word, it's no joke!
I need to find something
to eat – and real *quick*.

I'm feeling quite weak
    and terribly
        sick . . .

I'm **SO** <u>SO</u> FAMISHING
I'm vanishing!"

"Don't worry," said Bug.
"We'll find you some food.

Come, follow me – we'll soon change your mood."

So a mAHOOsive
breakfast was gulped
down in one.
But . . .

"Dear Mammoth," sighed Bug.
"You STILL look so glum."

"Perhaps," he said.
"You're in need of a snack."

And he pulled a banana
out from his knapsack.

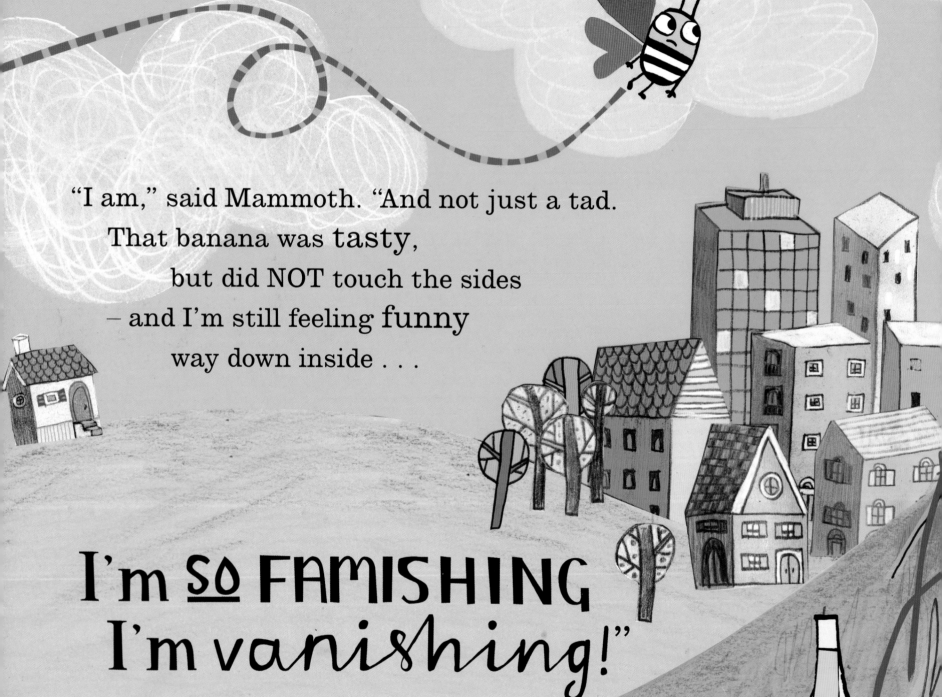

But when it had gone, Mammoth looked sad.
"What's the matter?" asked Bug.
"Are you still feeling bad?"

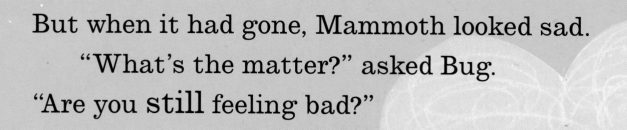

"I am," said Mammoth. "And not just a tad.
That banana was tasty,
but did NOT touch the sides
– and I'm still feeling funny
way down inside . . .

I'm SO FAMISHING
I'm vanishing!"

"Well," said Bug. "It's not time for lunch.
But perhaps you'll feel better
after some brunch?

Come, dear friend, just follow me."
And so Mammoth did . . .

. . . after gobbling a **tree!**

"Maybe," said Bug.
"We'll pass on brunch.
It's midday already,
so let's do lunch.

A hearty meal,
and then you'll feel fine,
my FAMISHING vanishing
BEST FRIEND of mine."

After lunch, Mammoth said,
"I just don't know how,
but my tummy is rumbling –
I could still eat a cow.

Lunch was five star
but did NOT touch the sides
and I'm still feeling funny
way down inside . . .

I'm SO FAMISHING I'm vanishing!"

By now, poor old bug was near out of ideas.
But it hurt to see Mammoth so close to tears. So . . .

"We are at the seaside," said Bug, with a grin. "An ice cream or doug

my FAMISHING *vanishing!* BEST FRIEND of mine."

They walked on the promenade and, on the wa

t will soon fill you in. A little sweet treat and then you'll feel fine —

ammoth munched much to keep hunger at bay —

doughnuts and ice cream, popcorn and chips. Candy floss, rock . . .

. . . and even a SHIP!

Lamp posts and bushes, shop fronts and signs –

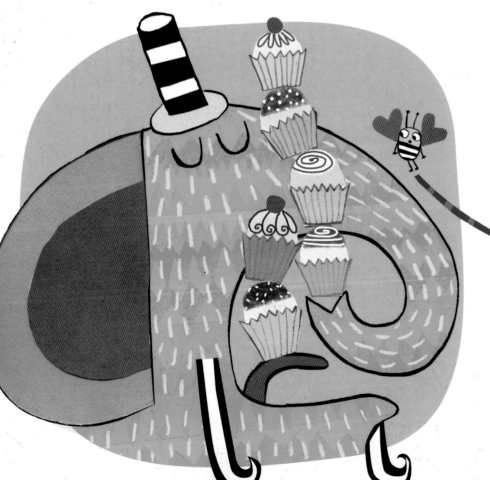

all manner of cupcakes
in different designs.

Until . . .

"My dear friend," said Bug. "This really must STOP.
I'm worried about you.
Your tummy will

POP!!

Your problem is this – if I might say –
you keep **thinking** of **food** ALL through the day.

We need to do something, to take your mind off it.
So, let's play a game of . . .

To moon **on** a ROCKET!

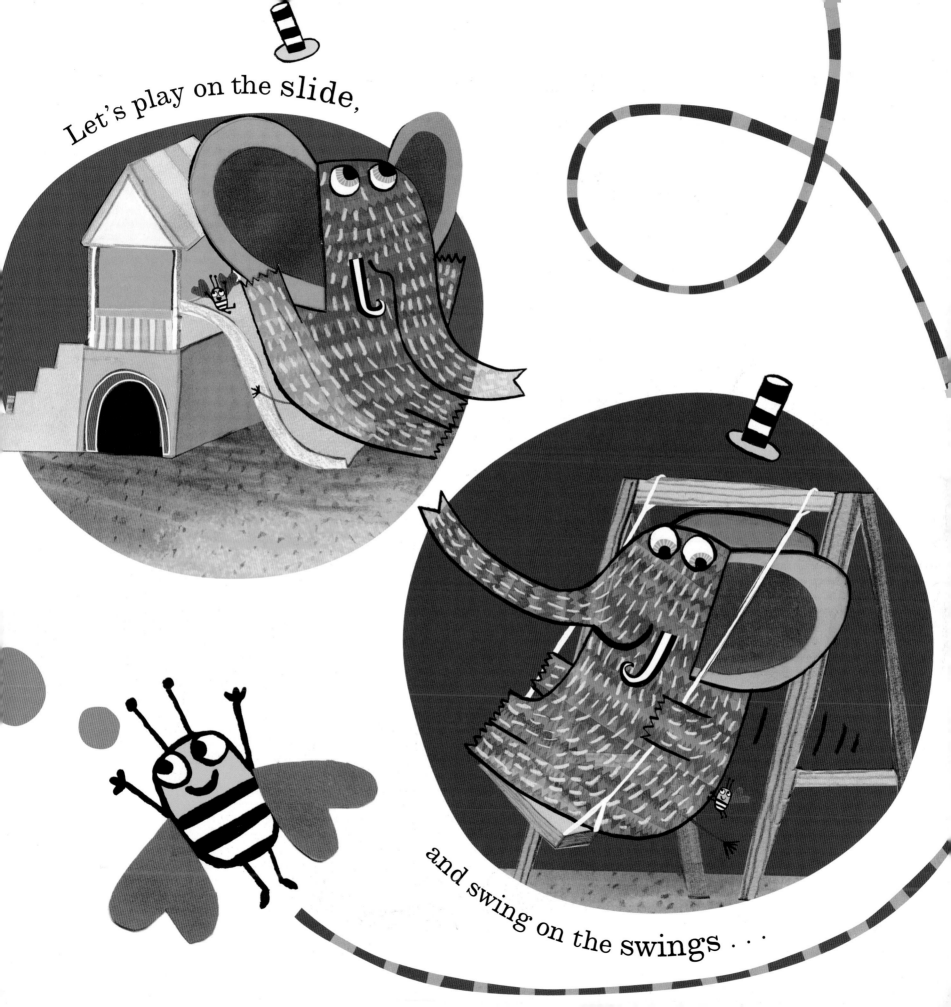

Let's play on the slide,

and swing on the swings . . .

. . . then find buried TREASURE; play castles and kings. '

So that's what the

id and boy was it fun! Not once did Mammoth think of his tum!

"Oh, Bug," said Mammoth. "You're such a GOOD friend.
I thought that my hunger never would end.

I'm much better now, yet there's something I need.
Something from YOU, Bug,
a real **friendly** deed.

It's NOT a snack or a morsel,
not a banquet or feast.
NOT a meal or a titbit
– it's **nothing** to eat.

There's one tiny thing
that will make me feel fine –
my generous
kind-hearted
BEST FRIEND
of mine.

A **hug** from a **bug** is the <u>ONE</u> THING I need."

And a hug from a bug
was most
gratefully
received.

For Sam, Nathan and Charlotte – H. H.

For little Jodi-Pie – L. H.

Bloomsbury Publishing, London, Oxford, New York, New Delhi and Sydney
First published in Great Britain in 2016 by Bloomsbury Publishing Plc
50 Bedford Square, London, WC1B 3DP

Text © Hollie Hughes 2016
Illustrations © Leigh Hodgkinson 2016
The moral rights of the author and illustrator have been asserted

A CIP catalogue record for this book is available from the British Library

ISBN 978 1 4088 6277 3 (HB)
ISBN 978 1 4088 6278 0 (PB)
ISBN 978 1 4088 6276 6 (eBook)

Printed in China by Leo Paper Products, Heshan, Guangdong

1 3 5 7 9 10 8 6 4 2

All papers used by Bloomsbury Publishing are natural, recyclable products made from wood grown in well-managed forests.
The manufacturing processes conform to the environmental regulations of the country of origin.

www.bloomsbury.com

BLOOMSBURY is a registered trademark of Bloomsbury Publishing Plc